Bedtime Meditation For Kids: Beautiful Yoga Nidras To Guide Your Kids To Dreamland

An assorted collection of dreamy visualization stories to help children reduce anxiety, relax and fall asleep fast.

- MINDFULNESS LIFESTYLE

Introduction

Kids nowadays grow up in very noisy environment. Electronic gadgets like the television and the smartphone have drained their imagination and creativity completely, making it harder for them to sleep.

Being people who work with children almost on a daily basis, we know how important visualization and meditation are for a child's mental health. Therefore, we created this book especially for today's children, who have trouble falling asleep.

This book will help them reconnect with their vivid imagination by making them visualize a peaceful dreamy story each night. Apart from the wonderful magical journeys, these stories also have important morals at the end. These morals make children feel grateful for all they have. Also, basic mindfulness techniques such as breathing and stretching have been integrated into each story to help children relax their mind and body.

These meditation stories are scientifically designed to get any child to slowly drift into the most amazing sleep of their life. There are a total of 5 dreamy visualization stories in this book, 1 for each night. These stories are supposed to be played when child is ready for bed and has their eyes closed.

The stories in this book use elements of life, nature, and magic along with beautiful background music and realistic sounds to make children feel like they are actually inside a dream. Although these stories written specifically for children, don't be surprised if you find yourself drifting off into deep sleep too!

We hope that your little one loves the book!

Table Of Contents

Sleep Journey 1 – Leo - The Majestic Dog

Settle back in your own comfortable bed, and close your eyes…

Take a deep breath in…

Hold the breath for the second… and now let it go…

Good…

Take another deep breath in…

And slowly… and gently, breathe out…

Feeling very relaxed…

Again, deep breath in… and slowly… and gently, breathe out…

Feeling very peaceful…

Very calm…

Now, take another deep breath in, this time lifting your arms slightly, and tightening them up…

As you breathe out, let your arms slump back down….

Just relax, letting go of all the tension in your muscles…

Again, breathe in…

Lift your arms slightly… and tense them up…

And breathe out, letting them drop back down…

Relax your whole body, letting go of all the tension in your muscles…

Now, follow the same procedure with your legs…

Take a deep breath in, raising your legs slightly, and tensing them up….

And as you breathe out, let them come back down again…

One more time, deep breath in…

Raise your legs, and tighten up those muscles…

And as you breathe out, let them down slowly …

Just relax and keep breathing slowly now…

.

.

[Pause]

.

.

Notice how your body feels…

Notice how soft your muscles are now…

It feels so good as you lie there….

Now, bring your breathing back to its normal rhythm…

Feel your body so relax…

Notice that your arms... and your legs have become heavier...

You don't really want to move them now...

That's okay...

That's good....

Let them rest...

Now imagine that there is a beautiful white light surrounding your whole body...

And this beautiful white light is beneath your feet, and above your head....

And you see it...

And you see it sparkle...

It feels like you are in a cocoon...

A cocoon of beautiful, safe, and healing energy....

And it looks as if you are glowing...

And this light will keep you safe from all of your worries....

It will keep you safe and protected, from any other problems that may be troubling you too...

Feel how relaxed you are...

How calm you are....

And how safe you feel, as this protective light surrounds your whole body, like an armor...

It can help you feel calm... feel relaxed...

.

.

[Pause]

.

.

Now, imagine that you are on a vacation...

A vacation to a hill station...

The place is surrounded by mountains with ice clad peaks...

You see big beautiful trees with fruits all around...

It is evening now...

You can feel the chill breeze ....

The moisture in the air...

There is dew on the leaves...

This hill station really is a good vacation from your home...

.

.

[Pause]

.

.

You decide to go for an evening walk...

You put on a thin sweater to feel cozy...

As you walk up and down the roads of the mountain, you feel more… and more relaxed…

You enjoy being in this weather…

You are free of any worry or tension…

Breathe in… and out…

You just enjoy the moment now…

.

.

[Pause]

.

.

As you walk along the hilly road, you see a dog sitting in the distance…

It is a beautiful brown dog…

You don't know what he is doing…

He seems to be lying down…

You can listen to it as it hauls…

He does seem to be in some sort of pain…

It looks like he is calling out for your help…

Feeling bad for him, you decide to go closer and help him out…

As you go closer, you see that the dog's leg is injured….

He can't walk properly…

It hurts him when he tries to walk….

You decide to take him to your place and apply some bandages at his wounds...

The dog is majestic, but adorable at the same time...

His eyes are dark brown and deep...

He looks strong... and caring...

You can see his love for you as you help him out...

You take him to your place, and apply bandages at his wound...

You give him his favorite food, and tell him to sleep with you for the night...

He tells you that he is so thankful to you...

He also tells you that his name is Leo...

"Leo...", what a beautiful name you think...

Leo is very happy now...

You can see the love in his eyes...

.

.

[Pause]

.

.

It is night time now, so both of you say goodnight to each other and try to go to sleep...

Half an hour passes by, and you don't seem to be able to go to sleep...

You are unable to sleep because of the sounds outside your house...

You are a little scared too...

But, you tell yourself that it is all in your head and try going to sleep...

Just as you drift a little into sleep, you hear a loud thud...

There are bad people trying to break into your house and steal things...

You are so scared that they might hurt you too...

You start to scream for help...

Just then, Leo jumps out and bites the thieves...

"Leo! Nooooo!", you are scared that they might hurt Leo...

But, Leo is a very strong dog...

He loves you a lot...

He will do anything to protect you...

The thieves run away in agony...

They are scared....

Leo chases them a little and drives them far away...

They would never come back now...

"Leoooo!! You protected me!", you scream...

You love Leo so much!

He protected you today...

He took care of you…

He was there when you needed him….

Leo jumps at you wagging his tail in joy!

You feel so happy…

Both of you eat some tasty fruits, and decide to go to sleep…

.

.

[Pause]

.

.

A friend in need is a friend indeed…

Remember this child…

True friends are always there for you when you need them…

You feel relived and relaxed now…

You are so happy that Leo and you are the best of friends now…

You hug Leo tightly…

And slowly start to drift into the most wonderful sleep…

Your body feel very relaxed….

Very peaceful…. and calm….

You are going deeper… and deeper, into a sound sleep…

So, rest now child….

A good peaceful night to rest…

And when you wake in the morning….

You will feel so refreshed…

Goodnight dear….

Sleep Journey 2 – A Journey To Outer Space

Gently close your eyes…

Now, shift your attention from your eyes to your nose…

Take a deep breath in through your nose, and exhale completely…

Take another deep breath in…

And slowly …and gently, breathe out through your mouth…

One more time…

Take a deep breath in…

And slowly… and gently, breathe out through your mouth…

And relax… feeling peaceful… and calm….

.

.

[Pause]

.

.

Now imagine a beautiful white bubble inside you….

A really, really small white bubble…

It is glowing…

The light inside it so bright…

But it doesn't hurt...

The light makes you feel warm... and protected...

The bubble is slowly growing bigger...

Bigger... and bigger...

It is almost as big as you now...

It is growing even bigger...

You are completely inside the bubble now...

The bubble will protect you.... and bring you peace ...

You feel warm and cozy...

You are free of any worries or tensions...

You feel so protected...

Breathe inside this glowing white bubble...

Feel the oxygen rich air, as it enters your body...

.

.

[Pause]

.

.

Now you are lying on your bed, relaxing....

All warm and cozy...

The weather is pleasant and the moonlight is bright...

The moonlight is so bright that it feels like your curtain is glowing...

It feels like a magical night...

You feel relaxed... and happy...

You feel like peeping out of the window to see the beautiful shiny moon...

So, you get out of your bed and draw the curtains to the side...

You see the huge silver moon glowing brightly in the clear night sky...

'Wooowwww! The moon never looked so beautiful...', you think to yourself...

It is so bright that you can actually see a bit of the scenery around...

You breathe in the fresh cool air...

You feel so relaxed and calm...

Keep breathing as you relax...

.

.

[Pause]

.

.

You look up at the night sky...

There are a million shining stars...

They are twinkling, as if they are calling you out...

You wish you could go to explore the stars and the moon...

Just as you are dreaming, you see an object with a trail, up in the sky....

Is it a meteor...? Or a rocket...?

You don't exactly know...

But you see it getting bigger and bigger...

Is it coming towards you...?

You look at it for a couple of seconds and realize that the object is indeed headed your way...

"Oh my god! Nooo!", you scream...

You are scared that this flying object may crash into your house...

Just then, you notice that the flying object slows down quite a bit...

Now, it is cruising slowly towards you...

And now it finally stop...

It is a huge white spaceship...

It looks like it is from the future...

You wonder why it came here...

You still are a little scared and confused...

Just then, you hear a soft, gentle, and caring voice...

The voice seems to be coming from inside the spaceship...

It says –

"Hello friend! We got to know that you were interested in visiting our land. Would you like to come along and have a fun little adventure?"

You obviously want to go, but you are not very sure because you are a little scared...

But, the voice is really calming and soothing...

It belongs to a very caring person, you think...

Also, you aren't very sleepy, so you decide to go...

You say –

"Yes! Take me along please!"

Just then, a platform from the spaceship gently lowers and comes close to your window...

It adjusts itself perfectly and then you hear the voice again...

"Step on it friend, don't worry... you are perfectly safe..."

So, you step on the platform, and it starts rising gently...

It starts rising gently towards the spaceship...

You are so excited...

You have a closer look at the spaceship...

It looks so modern. Rather futuristic.

You can't wait to see what the future has in store for you...

The platform then slowly takes you inside the spaceship...

You can see all sorts strange things inside...

There is also a very comfortable looking bed...and a sofa....and a television too....

"Unbelievable!", you think to yourself...

Just then, you hear the wonderful soothing voice again...

It is coming from the TV...

You see a strange looking creature on the screen...

It looks like a combination of an elephant and a parrot....

It has huge ears like an elephant and a big nose like a parrot's beak....

It looks like an alien...

But you find it cute...thanks to it ever so calming voice and smile...

It says −

"Hey there buddy! My name is elepharrot! Are you ready to begin your journey to the moon and outer space?"

"Woww!", you think to yourself...

You say yes...

You are damn excited...

The elepharrot then tells you to get comfortable and sit on the sofa....

You sit on the cushiony sofa and you see some seat belts coming across your body...

The seat belts tighten up just the right amount...

The elepharrot says −

"You are ready for the launch now... Please press the red button on the armrest of the sofa to begin your journey..."

Just then, you see a red button pop out on the armrest of the sofa...

You are so excited!

You press the red button and...

Oh my god...

You see the scenery around you moving so fast...

So fast that it is almost too hazy to tell what you see...

But, you don't feel a thing...

The spaceship and the sofa are really comfortable, and you barely feel that you are moving...

Soon, you see that you are high up into the night sky....

You are way above the clouds and the land....

You can see some stars really close to you....

The moon looks very big now!

You slowly start to feel a little weightless...

You feel really light!

You are into space now...

Just then, you hear the elepharrot again...

"Hi friend! You are into space now...You might want to play around and enjoy a little before you land on the Moon..."

You think that this is a really good idea!

So, you untie your seatbelt and start floating around in the spaceship...

It feels as if you are flying...

It feels so good...

It feels so magical....

You grab your spacesuit and decide to float around in space before you visit moon...

So, you wear your spacesuit, and open the spaceship's door...

And what you see, blows your mind....

"Beautiful!!", you exclaim...

You can see shiny golden stars and magical colourful trails everywhere!

Take some time to enjoy yourself here child...

Take a look around and float in outer space for a while...

.

.

[Pause]

.

.

Now that you have played around and have had a little fun, you decide to go back to the spaceship...

You find Elepharrot waiting there for you on the TV...

Elepharrot is delighted to see you all happy and cheerful...

He says, that now you can come to the Moon to visit him and his friends....

The moon doesn't seem very far away...

And with the incredible speed of the spaceship, it would barely take a minute to reach...

So, you buckle up, and get ready to launch the spaceship again....

You hit the red button, and the spaceship flies through space....

You can see the moon getting bigger and bigger....

It looks as like a huge silver ball with some dark spots on it....

You hear Elepharrot say that your spaceship would land in 15 seconds...

You look around and see a small red colored landing platform....

Your spaceship is now slowing down...

It is getting ready to land on the Moon...

And in just a few seconds, you hear a little thud...

Your spaceship has now touched down on the Moon!

This is unbelievable! You always wanted to visit the moon and the outer space...

You feel like you are inside a dream!

.

.

[Pause]

.

.

You see your friend, the Elepharrot, waving happily at you from outside the window of the spaceship...

You unbuckle yourself, and wear your spacesuit quickly...

Then, you open the door and see Elepharrot standing right outside...

Elepharrot is overjoyed seeing you!

You are no less excited!

You greet and hug each other!

Elepharrot tells you, that the moon is a home to a lot of different variety of aliens like himself...

He calls out his friend, the Girracock...

His friend resembles a giraffe and a peacock...

Elepharrot introduces you to Girracock...

Both of you greet each other, and then all three of you roam around in a car on the surface of the Moon...

.

.

[Pause]

.

.

You people then go to grab a drink and some snacks...

You have your favorite drink and snacks, and have a wonderful time with Elepharrot and Girracock...

Then, all three of you decide to go to their school...

You get to know that they are classmates and best friends...

You love spending time with both of them...

You wish you could come there and study with them!

Soon, you see a huge futuristic building with stunning bright lights...

It looks like a space station...

They tell you that this is their school...

They say that things are taught very differently here....

You are interested in knowing more about their school, so all of you go in to explore the school...

The first class you see is a drawing class...

You see some unique device in the hands of the children...

They are drawing lifelike pictures using this special device...

You then see the Math, English and all other classes too...

Everything seems so fascinating...

Everything is taught here so differently, you think to yourself...

Just then, you see an old alien walking by...

Your friends tell you that he is the principal of their school...

They say he is the sweetest alien ever... and that he is very wise...

You see the old alien walk into his room...

There is a giant student inside his room...

He looks half Dinosaur and half crocodile...

He is scary, but funny at the same time...

Your friends tell you that his name is Crocdino...

They say that he is the naughtiest student in the school...

All of you watch the principal as he begins to talk with Crocdino...

The principal politely asks Crocdino why he was sent to him again...

Crocdino says that he lied to the teacher, that's why he is here...

He lied about his homework...

The principal then takes him to a garden that is just outside his cabin...

The principal tells him to pluck a small leaf...

Crocdino pulls it out easily...

Then, the principal tells him to pull out the whole plant...

It takes a little effort, but Crocdino does that too...

Now, the principal tells Crocdino to pull out an entire tree...

Crocdino uses all his strength and might, but is unable to pull the tree out...

The tree stays firmly planted in the ground...

You don't seem to understand what's going on...

The principal then speaks up...

He says dear Crocdino...

These plants are like your habits...

It is easy to remove a bad habit early...

But when it settles inside you, it is as difficult to remove as it is to uproot a tree...

Now you understand why the principal made Crocdino do all this...

It all makes sense now...

The principal is so wise... and intelligent, you think to yourself...

Crocdino seems to understand his mistake...

He would never ever forget this lesson...

He promises to never lie again...

.

.

[Pause]

.

.

So child, get rid of your bad habits as soon as possible, otherwise it becomes very difficult to leave them...

.

.

[Pause]

.

.

You had a very interesting journey today...

It was a great adventure to the moon and outer space...

You made awesome new friends...

You also learnt a very important lesson from the wise principal today...

Now, you are starting to feel a little tired...

So, you tell your friends to drop you back to the spaceship...

Elepharrot and Girracock take you to the spaceship...

You promise to see them again really soon...

Elepharrot tells you that you can comfortably sleep in the spaceship, and it would drop you directly to your bed...

You are happy hearing this as you are really tired...

So, you bid them a goodbye, and start your journey back...

You press the red start button, and lie down in the comfortable spaceship bed, feeling really happy ... and relaxed...

The best part is that you can sleep here right now, and you would directly be in your bed when you wake up the next morning...

.

.

[Pause]

.

.

You will feel very refreshed and relaxed tomorrow morning when you wake up...

But for now, just enjoy the comfortable cushiony bed...

Snuggle down inside the comfortable blanket and take a deep breath in...

And let go...

You feel so relaxed...

And my guiding voice will now be leaving you, as you gently rest and start drifting into sleep...

.

.

[Pause]

.

.

Take a deep breath ...

And slowly breathe out...

Feel yourself becoming more... and more relaxed...

One more deep breath in...

And gently breathe out...

More... and more sleepy ...

More... and more peaceful...

Goodnight little one...

May you sleep well tonight...

Sleep Journey 3 – Wildlife Safari

Gently close your eyes...

Now, shift your attention from your eyes to your nose...

Take a deep breath in through your nose, and exhale completely...

Take another deep breath in...

And slowly ...and gently, breathe out through your mouth...

One more time...

Deep breath in...

And slowly... and gently, breathe out through your mouth...

And relax... feeling peaceful... and calm....

.

.

[Pause]

.

.

Now, imagine being surrounded by a beautiful white light...

This light surrounds your whole body...

It's beneath your feet, and above your head....

And you are inside this light...

Just like a caterpillar safe in its cocoon...

This light is very special...

And inside this light, you know that you are always safe...

And you know that you are always loved...

And you know that you are always protected...

.

.

[Pause]

.

.

Now imagine that you are in a jeep...

You are outdoors, exploring the wildlife...

It is a sunny day, you feel warm and cozy...

You are out on a safari in Africa's most wildlife rich grassland...

There are huge spans of grasslands all around...

The grass is brownish green in color...

The air around you is still ... and calm....

And you can hear different sounds of all the creatures...

Can you hear them?

.

.

[Pause]

.

.

The birds are flying high up into the sky...

You can hear the elephants calling out to each other...

Baby elephants are smiling seeing their mothers...

They are so cute...

You go to a baby elephant, and give it an apple...

The elephant is so happy seeing the apple...

She pulls in the apple through her trunk and eats it....

She hugs you with joy!

You ask the baby elephant her name...

She says her name is Klara...

She asks you your name...

You tell her your name...

You just made a new friend...

You are so happy!

.

.

[Pause]

.

.

Klara wants to play with you now...

You have a football with you in the jeep...

So, you bring the ball, and Klara gathers her friends...

She introduces you to her friends.... Edward the Zebra, Arnold the Giraffe, and Smokey the Hippo...

You say hi to them all, and then all you start playing...

Enjoy playing football with them...

Laugh and have fun...

.

.

[Pause]

.

.

After you are done playing, all of you sit down to eat some snacks and relax...

It is getting a little cooler now...

Just as all of you are having a great time relaxing, Edward the Zebra notices something...

His face turns pale, and he starts crying....

You ask him what's wrong?

He points to your right....

You see a lion approaching....

"OH NO!"

The lion looks very hungry …

Each one of you is scared…

Just then, Klara mother, Diana comes running…

She tells all of you not to worry and to stick together…

She says that the lion is waiting for you to run for that he can hunt you down one by one…

She says that when you are together, he can't hunt all 4 of you down at once, that is why he is not attacking…

You are a little relieved as Klara's mother is here, but no fully, as the lion is still looking at you…

Soon, the lion loses hope, and walks away…

All of you are so relieved now!

You thank Diana for coming just at the right time and sharing her wisdom…

.

.

[Pause]

.

.

You learnt a very important lesson today child…

Strength is in unity…

Staying together saved all of you today...

.

.

[Pause]

.

.

Now, your friends show you around the most beautiful places of the grassland...

You are delighted seeing some of the places...

Now, you and your friends decide to lie down on a grassy slope and close your eyes...

Don't worry, this place is safe...

Diana is also around, so there is no need to worry...

As you lie down on the soft, comfortable grass, a cool breeze blows by...

Diana gives all of you small blankets...

This feel just perfect...

You are getting a little sleepy now...

This feels as comfortable as your very own bed...

You also have your friends here...

You feel protected... and relaxed...

Breathe in... and out child...

Just relax...

Relax and let go of all worries...

Keep breathing...

Now, my guiding voice will be leaving you as you gently rest and start drifting into sleep....

.

.

[Pause]

.

.

Take a deep breath ...

And slowly breathe out...

Feel yourself becoming more... and more relaxed...

.

.

[Pause]

.

.

One more deep breath...

And gently breathe out...

More... and more sleepy ...

You feel really peaceful...

Goodnight little one...

Sleep Journey 4 – The Golden Castle

Find a nice comfortable place to lie down...

Or climb into your very own warm bed...

Lay your head on your pillow, and rest for a little while...

As you do so, take a deep breath in through your nose...

And slowly... and gently, breathe out through your mouth...

Take another deep breath in...

And slowly... and gently... breathe out through your mouth...

Keep breathing...

.

.

[Pause]

.

.

Again, take deep breath in ...

And slowly... and gently... breathe out through your mouth...

Relax now...

.

.

[Pause]

.

.

Now, take another deep breath in...

And as you do so, raise your shoulders up towards your ears...

Lift them up....

And as you exhale, let your shoulders slowly drop down again...

Relax...

Again, breathe in, lifting your shoulders high up towards your ears...

And breathe out, letting your shoulders drop back down again...

And relax....

Just bring your breathing back to its normal rhythm now...

.

.

[Pause]

.

.

Imagine that there is a beautiful white light around you...

It is surrounding your whole body...

A light of peace... and protection...

See how it sparkles...

See how it shines...

You can feel the warmth of this peaceful light as it surrounds you, making you feel so very safe... and protected...

.

.

[Pause]

.

.

Are you ready for today's adventure child?

Alright then, let's go to another magical place today...

Close your eyes and take a deep breath in...

Let's count till 10 in our minds, shall we? And when you wake up, you will be in the lands of your dream...

Breathe in and out slowly as we count till 10...

1...2...3...4...5... keep breathing ...6 ...7...8 ...9...10...

Now, you are lying on a green grassy slope of a river bank...

The grass underneath you is soft... and comfortable...

It is a warm sunny day...

You feel really comfortable and relaxed lying here...

In front of you is a large beautiful flowing river…

It is so clean and lively…

The weather is just perfect…

The scenery is so beautiful…

You just want to lie down here, and relax forever… in this complete calming silence…

.

.

[Pause]

.

.

On the other side of the river, you can see sheep grazing the lush green grass…

They seem to be so peaceful…

You are enjoying the surrounding…

So, you decide to relax for a while, and close your eyes…

As your eyes begin to close, you slowly start to see a huge golden castle appear in front of you on the other side of the river…

You think that this must be a dream…

Meanwhile, the castle continues to get more and more visible…

It is almost fully visible now….

You seem a little confused…

You open your eyes to see what's going on…

And as soon as you do that, you are taken aback…

"Oh my god!", you exclaim…

It really looks like there is a castle in front of you now…

You weren't dreaming after all…

A huge golden castle just appeared right in front of you, out of nowhere…

Are you in some magical world?

You don't know, but you sure are excited…

You just gaze at the huge golden castle for a couple of moments…

How does the castle look?

.

.

[Pause]

.

.

"The King must be really rich", you think to yourself, seeing the giant gold castle...

You really want to go into the castle and see what's inside, but the castle is on the other side of the mighty river...

You get up and walk a little closer to the river...

You are trying to figure out a way to reach the other side of it...

Just as you are thinking of a way to cross the river, a strong wide wooden bridge starts to appear...

You are surprised...

You now see the wooden bridge connecting you to the castle...

"Woww! What is happening!", you say to yourself...

You really want to go in and explore this magical castle...

So, you step on the bridge and start walking slowly towards the castle...

While walking, you can see how fast and lively the river is...

You feel some cold water splashing onto you...

It gives you chills...

You feel thrilled!

You love the place...

You are excited and happy...

.

.

[Pause]

.

.

As you walk towards the castle, you notice that there is something written on a big golden board...

You can't read it yet, but you see that something is written there...

So, you go closer to the board to take a look at it...

It says —

"Hello chosen one! Welcome to the castle of gold! The king is waiting for you inside! Hurry!"

You feel really special reading this...

You rush towards the entrance of the castle...

Now, you are on the other side of the river, in front of the big golden arched entrance of the castle...

You see the entrance leading to a long pathway inside the castle...

The board at the entrance says – 'Pathway to the King's throne"

So, you decide to go inside the castle...

You begin walking along the pathway...

The pathway is well lit with flames of either side...

You see photos of pigeons, pigeons of various age groups on either side of the wall...

Soon, you reach the end of the pathway...

You see a curtain, a big tall curtain...

You guess that the King's throne must be inside...

So, you open the curtain just a little bit...

And you see such a bright golden light that you instantly close your eyes and hide back behind the curtain...

You hear somebody say – "Oh, he is here!"

And just then, a pigeon pops his head out from the other side of the curtain...

He gives you some special glasses to wear, and then tells you to slowly come inside...

You wear the glasses, and step inside...

"Woww! Unbelievable!", you exclaim...

The bright golden light was because of the amount of gold in the hall...

Everything you could see was made of gold ... literally everything!

There was a huge gold throne in the centre of the hall...

On it, was sitting a majestic little pigeon with a golden cap on his head...

He must be the king, you think...

The king pigeon says hi to you, and tells you to introduce yourself...

You tell everybody your name and also told them how you ended up here...

The King pigeon then says that only a few selected people in the world see this magical gold castle...

Just as the king is telling you about his castle, an owl enters the hall through the curtains...

The bright golden light doesn't seem to hurt him at all...

He calmly walks in, and bows infront of the King...

The King says –

"You must be the famous magician I called..."

The owl gently nods his head...

He says – "Yes your majesty, I am the world-famous magician you called..."

The king pigeon is really greedy...

You already know that by the amount of gold he has in the hall...

So, the king pigeon says to the magician grinning –

"If you really are such an amazing magician, grant me the power to turn anything I think of, to gold..."

The magician Owl waits a couple of seconds, and then says –

"I can do that...But are you sure you want to possess such an incredible power...?"

The king says yes to him, and then the owl starts chanting a spell...

After a while, the owl says to the king that you possess the power to turn anything you think of, to gold...

The greedy king pigeon instantly thinks of the large curtain in the hall, and it turns to gold in a second!

"Oh my god!", the king pigeon exclaims...

He is overjoyed...

He is way too greedy, you think to yourself...

He has so much gold, but still wants more...

He wants to turn everything to gold...

He then thinks of the red carpet in front of him...

And that turns to gold too...

And then the wooden bridge turns to gold too...

And the grapes and other fruits in the basket near him too!

The basket itself...

His clothes...

Anything and everything he thinks of turns to gold...

What an extreme power to possess...

The king is so overexcited that he wants to tell the queen about his new power...

So, he thinks of the Queen to call her...

And, you know what happens next...

The queen turns to gold too...

"Oh no! What have I done! What has just happened! Oh no!", and the king pigeon bursts into tears...

He made his own queen into a gold statue because of his greed…

The owl then says that he warned the King about it…

But, because of his excessive greed, the king couldn't think properly…

The king begs the owl to reverse back everything…

He promises that he would never be greedy again…

The owl thinks that the King has learnt his lesson, and so, he reverses everything back to normal…

On seeing his Queen okay again, the King bursts into tears…

He promises to never be greedy ever again…

He realises his mistake…

.

.

[Pause]

.

.

Today you learnt a very important lesson child…

One should never ever be greedy…

One should always be happy and content with what one has…

.

.

[Pause]

.

.

Now, it is time for you to go back to your home...

You are feeling sleepy now...

The King offers you to sleep in his very own bedroom...

He says that his bedroom has a very special bed as it can make anyone wake up anywhere in the morning...

You are happy hearing about this...

You decide to wake up in your own bed the very next morning...

But for now, you decide to go to his bedroom, and sleep there...

.

.

[Pause]

.

.

You gently lie down on the bed and wrap a blanket around yourself...

You feel smarter and wiser today...

You learnt a very important lesson...

You are also very happy because the king and his queen are all okay now…

You are glad that the king understood his mistake and you also got to learn from it…

Now, it's time for you to grab some wonderful sleep child…

Feel every part of your body relax, as you snuggle down inside the comfortable blanket…

Take a deep breath in… and breathe out…

.

.

[Pause]

.

.

Deep breath in… and slowly … and gently, breathe out…

One more time, deep breath in… and slowly… and gently, breathe out…

.

.

[Pause]

.

.

Feel yourself becoming more... and more relaxed...

Take another deep breath in...

And gently breathe out...

Relax.... relax...

You are becoming more... and more sleepy ...

You feel so peaceful...happy...and content...

.

.

[Pause]

.

.

Goodnight child...

Have a wonderful sleep...

Sleep Journey 5 – Helping The Sheep

Close your eyes and make yourself comfortable...

.

.

[Pause]

.

.

Now, gently shift your attention from your eyes to your nose...

Take a slow, deep breath in through your nose...

And slowly... and gently, breathe out through your mouth...

Again, breath in deeply through your nose...

And slowly... and gently, breathe out through your mouth...

One last time, take deep breath in...

And gently breathe out...

.

.

[Pause]

.

.

Now, bring your breathing back to its normal rhythm...

Feel your chest rise... and fall gently....

You feel peaceful.... and calm....

You feel very relaxed....

And with each breath you take, you can feel yourself becoming more, and more relaxed....

And your body feels quite floppy...

It feels loose... and relaxed...

And you feel so calm now...

You feel so light...

You feel so very happy...

.

.

[Pause]

.

.

So child, are you ready for yet another amazing adventure today?

Alright then, let's go to dreamland!

Okay, so close your eyes and just listen to what I say...

Let's begin..

Slowly stretch your legs and arms...

And feel your body sinking into the bed…

Count till 10 in your mind…

Breathe in and out slowly as you count till 10…

1…2…3…4…5… keep breathing …6…7…8 …9…10…

You are now lying down on the soft green grass of a large green field…

This green field is on top of a mountain…

The weather today is perfect…

The sun is big, warm and friendly, and is shining brightly through the fluffy clouds…

It's a very beautiful, clear day…

You can see for miles ahead…

You feel very calm… very relaxed…. and ever so peaceful…

.

.

[Pause]

.

.

You see beautiful white birds flying over your head…

You can hear them singing…

Can you hear them…?

The chirping of birds makes you feel very close to nature...

.

.

[Pause]

.

.

You look up in the sky to find a beautiful colorful rainbow...

The colors are so bright... and clear...

Can you see it...?

How does it look?

Can you see how the colors sparkle... and shine...?

Can you see how the colors look almost alive...?

.

.

[Pause]

.

.

You look down the mountain... and see many horses running happily on the flat grassy-land in the distance...

You are so happy seeing them...

You want to meet those horses!

As you admire the horses in the distance, the rainbow suddenly glows...

You look at the rainbow...

It truly is the most beautiful rainbow you have ever seen...

You notice that the rainbow leads to the grassy lands where the horses are...

The rainbow glows again...

This is strange...

It almost feels like the rainbow is calling out to you...

What a magical rainbow, you think...

You feel so drawn to this amazing rainbow, that you decide walk towards it...

So, you start walking towards the magical rainbow...

.

.

[Pause]

.

.

As you get closer, you notice your steps becoming lighter... and lighter ...

It's almost feels as if you are floating towards the rainbow...

It feels like your feet are not even touching the ground now...

You feel so light...

Just as you are about to reach the rainbow, you stop...

You decide to take a good look at the rainbow...

It's then that you realize, that the rainbow is moving...

"Oh goodness me!", you exclaim...

You walk a little more today the rainbow, and it stops moving...

You step onto the rainbow, and as soon as you step onto it, it begins to move again...

It moves forward and begins to climb higher up into the sky...

And it climbs higher... and higher...

You see a beautiful sight of the whole place from the rainbow...

It feels like a dream...

You can even touch the colors of this rainbow...

What does it feel like to touch the rainbow...?

How does everything look...?

Breathe in the fresh air around you...

Keep breathing as you relax...

.

.

[Pause]

.

.

The rainbow starts to go even higher...

You can see the green grassy field below...

You can see many trees...

You can see the birds flying...

There are even a couple of them flying past your rainbow...

Can you see them...?

.

.

[Pause]

.

.

The rainbow now reaches its topmost height, and begins to move back down again...

Now, it's starting to get a bit slippery....

So, you decide to sit down....

And as you do so, you begin to slide...

Oh dear! You are sliding down the rainbow!

The rainbow is like a big waterslide... with beautiful colors all over....

You are now going faster... and faster...

The wind is whipping through your hair, making it fly everywhere...

This makes you laugh out loud...

Enjoy the slide...

.

.

[Pause]

.

.

You can see the end of the rainbow now, and it's coming fast...

You notice that at the bottom of the rainbow, there appears to be a huge trampoline...

Oh my! You are going to hit the trampoline so fast...

And you hit it... and then bounce right back up, and then back down... then right back up again!

This is so much fun!

You keep bouncing for a few minutes, up and down...

Enjoy!

.

.

[Pause]

.

.

After a while, you decide to get off the trampoline, onto the ground...

Just then, one of the horses stops and comes to you...

His name is Brown...

He seems pretty desperate for something...

He asks you if you can help them out...

You are a very good child, and so, you decide to help Brown out...

Hearing this, Brown smiles gracefully and tell you to follow him...

You then get up onto Brown and ride him to huge farmhouse....

Look around you...

Look at the lush green grass and the bushes...

Truly peaceful...

Breathe in the fresh air as it flows past you...

The air is so full of oxygen...

You feel complete...

Enjoy the ride and keep breathing...

.

.

[Pause]

.

.

Soon, you reach the farmhouse...

It has many animals...

Sheep, chickens, pigs, horses and many others too...

You are surprised seeing so many different animals living together...

Brown then takes you to the head of the farm, a dog named Tom...

Tom tells you that the sheep are out of control...

He says that they are not listening to him....

That they are disturbing all the other animals...

You really want to help them out...

So, you decide to go to the sheep and ask them why they are not listening to Tom...

The Sheep say that they do not want to work...

That they just want to play the whole day....

And they start playing again...

Looking at the Sheeps, the Pigs also start playing...

There are so many animals playing that it looks like an absolute madhouse...

While playing, a little sheep, Nick, gets hurt....

Nick the sheep needs help, but since everyone is playing, no one looks at him....

He starts to cry...

Soon, the other sheep and pigs also start to get hurt... and they start crying....

All of them are very hungry too, as they have been playing for quite a while...

So, you being a very good boy take the injured ones to the hospital... and bring food for the hungry ones...

You help as many of them as you can...

Just as you are helping out the animals, Tom the dog arrives...

He tells all the animals of the farmhouse why he told them all not to play at the same time...

He tells them that they must work as well....

"We must obey our elders", he says...

The sheep and pigs agree, and sit down quietly...

Everybody has their food is being taken care of now …

No one is crying…

Everyone is happy now…

Now, the sheep work first and then play….

They listen to Tom, their head…

Everyone is happy now….

Now that everything is good, you decide to lie down on the lush green grass and take some rest…

Everyone is happy and peaceful….

This makes you feel really good….

You helped everyone…

.

.

[Pause]

.

.

After some time, you see that Brown, the horse comes to you…

He says-

"You helped make this farm a peaceful place again! Thank you so much!"

.

.

[Pause]

.

.

Don't you feel good child...?

You helped others today...

Everybody is so happy because of you...

You should be proud of yourself....

You are a very good child...

.

.

[Pause]

.

.

Now, it is time to go to sleep...

A relaxing deep sleep...

Take a deep breath.... and exhale....

Feel the wind.... look at the big white clouds above you....

Relax...

.

.

[Pause]

.

.

Feel yourself sinking into the bed... getting cozy...

Take a deep breath in... and slowly... and gently, breathe out...

.

.

[Pause]

.

.

Take another deep breath in... and slowly ... and gently, breathe out...

Feel yourself becoming more... and more relaxed...

More... and more sleepy ...

So peaceful....

Goodnight little one...

Sleep like you never have!

Thank You!

Thank you for buying our book. If your child liked it, please let us know by dropping a review. It would be a pleasure and an encouragement to hear from you. If your child really enjoyed the unique idea of meditation stories, you could go ahead and buy another one of our fantastic books in the same "Magical Sleep" series, called the "Bedtime Stories For Children: Beautiful Yoga Nidras To Guide Your Kids To Dreamland.".

So, that's all for this book. Goodbye and have a great day!

Made in United States
Orlando, FL
01 November 2022